WAR WITHOUT ORDERS

THE FIRST STRIKE

War Without Orders
© 2025 Dr. Subin Mathews

This is a work of fiction. Names, characters, organisations, places, events, and incidents are either the product of the author's imagination or used fictitiously. Any resemblance to actual persons, living or dead, or actual events is purely coincidental.

Cover design by Dr. Subin Mathews

First Edition

DEDICATION

For the shadows that watch over us.

For those who fight in silence.

For those who protect what cannot be spoken of.

THE ORDER PROTOCOLS

A Political Thriller Series

In a world where diplomacy fails in silence and wars begin without orders, shadow operatives, fractured democracies, and collapsing regimes fight to control what the world is told—and what it never sees.

Each book in The Order Protocols series explores the layers beneath modern conflict:
covert intelligence, psychological warfare, betrayal from within, and the quiet decisions that shift history.

Book One: War Without Orders

A nation grieves. A shadow strike bypasses government.
And a nuclear-armed enemy believes it's winning—until silence turns into fire.

Book Two: Ashes of Order (Coming Late 2025)

With the war spiralling beyond control, enemies rise from within.
One spy. One lie. One rogue weapon—ready to rewrite the balance of power.

Table of Contents

Chapter 1 – The Quiet Mandate
A devastating terror attack rocks Suryadesh, but its leaders choose
diplomacy over retaliation at least on the surface.

Chapter 2 – The Mandate of Fire
As the public demands justice, Prime Minister Aditya Rao
prepares a national address. In the shadows, NSA Aarav Sen
initiates a covert plan.

Chapter 3 – Al-Bashir
Across the border, intelligence chief Zameer Qadir celebrates a
strategic victory, even as his regime begins to crack from within.

Chapter 4 – The Prime Minister's Burden
Aditya faces a divided cabinet, global pressure, and growing
unrest while Aarav expands operations without informing him.

Chapter 5 – The Man with the Camera
Journalist Karan Pratap boards a train to report the truth, only to
find the truth moving faster than the media can track.

Chapter 6 – Smoke Before Fire
Tensions flare as Al-Bashir fans the flames of misinformation,
and internal dissent begins to stir within Suryadesh.

Chapter 7 – The Vice Admiral's Interlude

The military waits. Orders don't come. Everyone watches, and no one acts... yet.

Chapter 8 – The Mirror of Desire

Tara Mehta, a respected diplomat, finds herself in a private encounter that will later be used to bring her down. At the same time, Al-Bashir deploys a honeytrap in Suryadesh's inner circle.

Chapter 9 – The Straw

Mobile terrorists unleash a brutal massacre on civilians. The death toll and national fury rise beyond restraint.

Chapter 10 – The Celebration

In Bashirat, Zameer hosts a party full of drugs, alcohol, and arrogance, as his people dance over the blood they spilled.

Chapter 11 – The Mourning

Suryadesh grieves its dead. Funerals, firetrucks, and folded flags weigh heavier than speeches.

Chapter 12 – Quiet Before Thunder

Aarav sets Operation Garuda in motion while Aditya tries and fails to win cabinet support for a retaliatory strike.

Chapter 13 – When Fire Falls

Missiles hit Al-Bashir. Zameer loses a critical base. Aditya realises too late that Aarav acted without him.

Chapter 14 – Ripples Through Glass

The global media reacts. Misinformation swirls. Within Suryadesh, emotions simmer into a call for vengeance.

Chapter 15 – The Counterfire
Al-Bashir retaliates with drones and sabotage. Suryadesh's defence holds, but the war shifts into a new phase.

Chapter 16 – The Second Wave
SIA plans a shadow campaign: destroy propaganda hubs, economic pipelines, and psychological strongholds.

Chapter 17 – Ghosts in the Feed
The narrative collapses. Suryadesh's people, once restrained, now demand retribution. Zameer loses the digital war.

Chapter 18 – The Rift
Aditya and Aarav face off. Words are exchanged. Trust erodes. Control of the war and the government is in question.

Chapter 19 – The Bait
An assassination attempt targets Aditya, Aarav, and the Defence Minister. They survive. Someone close to Aditya doesn't.

Chapter 20 – Shadowfront
Suryadesh launches coordinated, high-precision strikes on Al-Bashir's infrastructure without touching innocent lives.

Chapter 21 – Shadows Within
A nationwide sweep uncovers sleeper cells. One operative escapes: Leena. She was never supposed to survive this long.

Chapter 22 – Below the Threshold

Aarav discovers all of Al-Bashir's nuclear bunkers and prepares to strike. Meanwhile, Leena delivers new intel to Zameer.

Chapter 23 – The Trigger

Suryadesh hits the underground nuclear sites. Radiation is contained, but panic erupts. Zameer loses control.

Chapter 24 – Fracturelines

Zameer's government begins to collapse. Allies withdraw. Generals turn away. His empire is a shell.

Chapter 25 – The Knife Inside

Leena returns to Suryadesh with proof of an internal betrayal. Tara Mehta uncovers the true origin of her leaked sex tape. A rogue nuclear device is moving. And a message is received: **"Phase Two is green. The knife is already inside."**

PREFACE

This is a work of fiction.
While the nations of Suryadesh and Al-Bashir are imaginary, the geopolitics, disinformation tactics, media manipulation, and war strategies are inspired by real-world events and historical parallels.
This book is not about countries. It is about choices… those made in rooms without light, without law, and sometimes without orders.

— Dr. Subin Mathews

Prologue

No name. No flag. No map marker.

The men inside called it Point 427.

The world called it nothing, because it didn't exist.

It wasn't listed in any peace treaty. No journalist had ever visited. Even the smuggled satellite images were deleted 90 seconds after viewing.

And yet, inside that compound, operations were planned.
Radicals trained. Weapons filtered.
Messages sent : encrypted in poetry, sermons, and radio static.

At 03:14 hours, the sky shimmered once.
No roar. Just a compression of air, like the planet itself had held its breath.

Then came the fire.

It didn't fall from the sky.
It bloomed from within, from a depth designed for deniability.

Point 427 ceased to exist before the first man inside could blink.

Bones turned to steam.
Steel to gravel.

In Suryadesh, the radar screens stayed blank.
No enemy strike. No official report.

Only a closed-loop transmission from an unnamed drone
operator:

> "Point 427—neutralised. No attribution. No footprint."

Across the border, in Al-Bashir, Zameer Qadir stared at a blank
square on a satellite feed.

He tapped his cigarette twice and whispered:
"They've started."

WAR WITHOUT ORDERS

Chapter 1 – The First Whisper

Surya Nagar – January 17, 02:34 hrs

Private Residence of the National Security Advisor

The steam from the tea had long gone cold.

Aarav Sen sat in the study, staring at a faded photograph on the wall. It showed him, twenty years younger, standing on a mountain ridge with two officers, all of them wrapped in army-issue parkas, snow in their beards, pride in their eyes. One of those men had died later that year. The other had lost his leg. Aarav had survived though some nights, he questioned what exactly had survived.

His wife had left the tea beside him at midnight. She hadn't knocked she knew his rhythms. Knew when to speak, and when to let silence sit beside him like a second shadow.

The room was still, save for the soft hum of the heater and the occasional wind pressing against the glass windows of their government bungalow. Outside, Surya Nagar slept.

The city didn't know that something was already broken.

Aarav's phone vibrated once. Not the usual ringtone. Not from any contact stored publicly.

He picked it up, heart steady, mind already working.

"Point 427 is offline," said a voice. Calm. Flat. No frills.

Aarav sat up straighter. "Technical?"

"No storm. No grid issue. Our thermal feed's gone too. Blackout across all channels."

He didn't answer for a moment.

Point 427 wasn't just any border post. It was a high-altitude listening station near the disputed ridge what the military called a "quiet ear." If it had gone dark, either someone had silenced it, or something far worse had happened.

"I want live drone feed. Thermal overlay. Call me back in fifteen," Aarav said.

"Sir… there's more. A pattern of signal distortion from thirty minutes before the blackout. We think it might be an EMP pulse."

"Where's the source?"

"Unknown. But too precise to be natural."

Aarav didn't thank him. He simply hung up.

He stood, stretched his back slowly, and walked to the window. The skyline of Surya Nagar was veiled in fog. Streetlights flickered in patches. Somewhere out there, behind the government buildings and sleepy embassies, was Sudarshan Hill the political heart of Suryadesh. By morning, the headlines would be about a peace conference in Vienna. Talks with Al-Bashir. Again.

He had read the PM's speech earlier that night: restraint, dignity, history, hope.

All things that Aarav, in his private heart, believed in.

But he also believed in timing. And tonight, something had shifted.

Twenty minutes later, Aarav entered the National Security Secretariat. The guard outside didn't ask questions. They never did when it was him.

Inside, he keyed in the override codes for the crisis room. The big screen on the far wall flickered to life, showing satellite feeds and a static overlay from Point 427. No movement. No heat. Just… absence.

A file sat on his desk, delivered by encrypted drop. It bore a single stamped word:

He opened it. Inside: one page.
A time stamp. A note on signal loss. A probable cause.

And a question handwritten in blue pen by someone senior:

"Sabotage… or invitation?"

Aarav closed the file and leaned back in his chair.

The Prime Minister was likely asleep. A man of discipline. So
was the Defence Minister a decorated soldier turned statesman,
still revered in uniformed circles. The new Foreign Secretary had
just returned from Europe and was optimistic. The SIA Surya
Intelligence Agency was cleaner than it had ever been. Focused.
Precise. Loyal.

But none of that mattered when the system beneath them moved
like cold molasses. Orders took hours. Signatures took days. And
the military calm, coiled, and powerful waited without protest,
while terror kept crossing the border in trucks marked with fruit.

Aarav knew how close they all were to tipping.

Not because anyone wanted war but because even patience bleeds
when it waits too long.

He dialled a secure number.

"I need flight clearance for the PM, Defence, and Foreign Secretaries."

"Sir?"

"They'll be attending separate conferences in different countries. Unofficial. Low-key."

"Why now?"

Aarav stared at the dead feed of Point 427.

"Because silence has weight," he said softly. "And this one feels heavy."

Chapter 2 – The Waiting Uniform

Sudarshan Hill, Suryadesh – January 17, 08:10 hrs

War Strategy Room, Vajra Command, Suryadesh Armed Forces Headquarters

Major General Devraj Malhotra stood perfectly still, even as the holographic map flickered on the wall behind him.

His crisp olive-green uniform was spotless, the brass on his shoulders polished to a mirror shine. Yet, beneath the calm exterior, his jaw clenched in silent rhythm. Tap. Release. Tap. Release.

Three hours ago, the command feed from Point 427 had gone silent.

Two hours ago, a special briefing had arrived from the National Security Secretariat marked **Eyes Only: Command Level.** He had read it three times. There was nothing new in the content. What struck him was what was **not** in the file.

No recommendation. No follow-up directive. No mobilisation notice.

Just acknowledgment of the silence.

Like they were expected to wait.

The war room buzzed with quiet motion around him. Young officers stared at screens, analysts hunched over satellite imagery. Data moved fast. Decisions did not.

Brigadier Sheela Verma, head of Strategic Surveillance, stepped beside him with a tablet.

> "No new recon from the Sat-3 array. Drone sent at 03:45 lost visual range halfway in. Could be jamming. Could be something else."

"Could be a graveyard," Devraj replied flatly.

Sheela nodded. "We've already prepped contingency orders. If this was an attack, we'll need go-ahead for air support in the northern ridge by nightfall."

"And do we have that go-ahead?"
Sheela didn't answer. She didn't have to.

They both knew the answer.

Devraj turned and looked through the thick glass wall facing the central courtyard. The flags flew high. Young cadets jogged in a morning drill. A peacetime rhythm. A country not yet told that its borders were bleeding.

He had spent his entire adult life serving under doctrine. Not ideology. Not emotion. Just structure.

But even doctrine had its limits.

He turned to the junior liaison officer nearby. "Any word from the NSA's desk?"

"Nothing formal, sir. Just that he's 'aware' and watching developments."

Devraj exhaled slowly through his nose. "Of course he is."

He respected Aarav Sen respected his cold brilliance, his stillness under pressure. But sometimes, brilliance could become a bottleneck.

And the army didn't like bottlenecks.

Far away, across the Suryadesh border, the news was already spinning a different narrative.

Al-Bashir's state network claimed a **"border provocation" by Suryadesh drones.** No visuals. No proof. Just bold letters and patriotic music. Their president, a former colonel now puffed up with propaganda, had promised a "swift and unforgiving response to any intrusion."

Devraj had seen it all before. The bravado of a failed state held up by loans, religion, and a careful scaffolding of chaos.

The only thing more dangerous than a strong enemy was a weak one pretending to be strong.

Sheela leaned in, voice lowered. "General… the men are restless. Quiet sectors report chatter. The border regiments want clarity."

Devraj turned to her, finally letting the tension leak through his eyes.

> "They want orders. So do I. But there's a chain we follow."
> "And what if the chain is tangled in silence?"

He didn't respond.

Because she had said the one thing no officer dared say aloud: What if war had already started but the decision-makers were still **waiting to write it down?**

He walked back to his seat, past polished granite walls and framed photos of battles fought by men with fewer tools and more courage.

He sat, and said softly perhaps to himself, or to the ghosts of Point 427:

> "We trained for a war with missiles and maps.
> But this one will be fought in waiting rooms.
> In silence. In delay.
> And maybe… without orders."

Chapter 3 – The Fire They Feed

Bashirat, Al-Bashir – January 17, 06:00 hrs

Presidential Palace, Al-Bashir

The room smelled of imported rosewood and old sweat.

President Umar Zakari sat alone at the edge of a long, lacquered table meant for thirty men. But only four chairs were occupied two generals, one minister, and an intelligence chief who preferred to remain unnamed in public documents.

A screen on the far wall played a muted clip from their national news network: a swirling graphic of Suryadesh's flag, superimposed with a red X, and below it, bold headlines in Urdu:

"SURYADESH DRONE PROVOCATION: POINT 427"

Zakari adjusted his collar. It was too tight, even though the tailor had taken his neck measurement just two days ago. Maybe it wasn't the collar. Maybe it was the truth tightening around his government like a slow noose.

He cleared his throat.

"Any confirmation they're aware it was us?"

The intelligence chief leaned forward. His voice was calm, but every word felt dipped in ice.

"They're aware something happened. But not how. Not yet."

Zakari grunted. "Not good enough. They'll guess. And when they do "

"They'll hesitate," said General Haroun, the Chief of Staff. "They always do. Their democracy is slow. Their peace faction is still in control."

"Until it isn't," Zakari muttered. "Until someone there finds his spine."

He stood, walked toward the window, and parted the curtains.

From this angle, Bashirat looked peaceful. The early call to prayer echoed in the distance, low and haunting. Traffic was light. The sun hadn't risen yet, but the sky was softening shifting from black to a warm rust. Morning made everything look cleaner than it was.

He closed the curtain.

"How long before the media turns this into another martyr story?" he asked.

The Minister of Interior shrugged. "The footage is already circulating. We'll inflate the death toll. Say our troops were attacked in their sleep. Burn a few fatigues and stage a funeral. Blame it on a Suryadesh border incursion."

Zakari said nothing. It was routine. Theatre.

It didn't matter how Point 427 went dark. What mattered was the opportunity.

His country was bleeding economically broken, diplomatically isolated, but strategically priceless. The West needed access. The East needed proximity. No one wanted stability; they wanted leverage.

And Al-Bashir had always played the perfect unstable ally.

He returned to his seat.

"How are the networks?" he asked.

The intelligence chief hesitated. "Restless. Some are going off-script. One commander in Kalat-al-Nur said he wants to act without waiting for us."

Zakari narrowed his eyes. "Remind him who signs his pay. And remind his mullah that we still control the mosques where he preaches."

He turned to General Haroun.

"I want visibility on all foreign consulates. If any of them begin evacuating staff, I want to know first."

Haroun nodded.

"And the money?" Zakari asked, now looking to his Finance Minister, who had remained silent until now.

"The Redvale Union payment has been delayed. Again."

Zakari's knuckles tapped the table softly. "And Jinzhou?"

"They're watching. They've promised support if we maintain plausible deniability."

Zakari's smile didn't reach his eyes. "Plausible deniability. The new opium."

He leaned back in the chair.

"Let's be clear," he said slowly. "If they strike back, we win. Our martyrs will rise. Their civilians will scream. The UN will call for calm. We'll cry foul. And in the end, we'll still get the aid."

No one spoke.

Zakari's voice dropped lower.

"But if they don't strike… if they hold back, like they always do… then we escalate again. Quietly. Sharper. Maybe even inside Surya Nagar this time."

The room felt colder.

This wasn't war for him. This was business. A balancing act of death and diplomacy.

The intelligence chief finally spoke again.

"There is one more thing. Our backchannel the one we had with that former Suryadesh general through Istanbul? It's gone cold."

Zakari frowned. "Did he run?"

"Maybe. Or maybe someone on their side found out."

Zakari tapped the table again.

"Find out who's cleaning their house. And tell our boys in Ummah-9 to lay low for now. No strikes without my approval. Let the media play its part first."
He stood again. Straightened his cuffs.

"Make them bleed. But only on paper. For now."

Chapter 4 – The Weight of Restraint

In-Flight – January 17, 11:45 hrs

Suryadesh One – En Route to Saphinia Peace Summit

Prime Minister Aditya Rao disliked flying.

Not because he feared it he had survived much worse but because it was one of the few times in his job that he was forced to sit still.

No aides. No rallies. No committee papers dropped into his lap mid-sentence. Just the hum of the engines, the dry cabin air, and the quiet roar of the altitude pressing against his thoughts.

He looked out the window. A thick quilt of clouds stretched beneath them, white and peaceful. Unbothered by borders.

If only countries could float above the mess they made.

Across from him, Foreign Secretary Tara Mehta was going over her summit notes. Meticulous, sharp, always a step ahead. She had been the one who insisted he personally attend the Saphinia Peace Summit a conference of middle powers seeking to reduce regional tensions.

"They'll be watching what you say more than what you sign," she had said. "And what you don't say, most of all."

Aditya nodded to himself now, thinking back on that. Every silence, every pause, every deflection would be analysed in every newsroom and embassy on Earth.

And meanwhile… **Point 427 was still silent.**

He leaned back and let his mind wander to the call he had received from Aarav before boarding.

> "I've ensured the extraction is seamless. If things move faster than we expect, you'll be in the clear."

Aarav had said it plainly, without drama. But Aditya knew what that meant.

They were preparing for a war without formally declaring one. A war that would begin from silence, not speeches.

Tara looked up from her tablet. "You haven't read the speech I drafted."

"I have," Aditya replied. "It's good. Firm. Hopeful. Just naïve enough to be admired."

She gave him a tight smile. "And your version?"

"I'll improvise. Depending on how much truth I think they deserve."

She studied him carefully. "Do you still believe peace can hold?"

He thought about that. Not just about Al-Bashir, or Zakari's games, or the global hypocrisy that let terror be subcontracted through aid packages but about the country he led.

His own people were starting to ask difficult questions. Why the restraint? Why the silence? Why the bodies in uniform kept coming home, draped in the tricolour, while ministers continued lighting ceremonial lamps at peace forums?

He had held the line for years.
But he knew this one might break.

"I believe peace is a privilege," Aditya finally said. "But it should never be mistaken for weakness."

Tara nodded slowly. "That's a good line. Use it tonight."

"I might."

The cabin door opened. A senior aide stepped in, hesitating before speaking.

"Sir, the Chief of Defence Staff sent an encrypted note. He says there's movement in the Dandaka Sector. Drones picked up vehicles unmarked."

Tara looked up sharply. Aditya closed his eyes briefly, then opened them.

"Where's Aarav?"

"He's already coordinating fallback. SIA has increased cyber activity across the border. Trinetra is watching for retaliatory proxies."

Aditya nodded. "Tell him not to blink. But not to speak either. Not yet."

The aide left. Silence returned.

Tara leaned forward.

"Do we retaliate if this escalates?"

Aditya met her gaze. "No. Not from me. Not from Parliament. Not through sound bites."

She tilted her head. "Then how?"

He looked back out the window.

> "When war comes, Tara… it must feel like an accident.
> Like a corner we were forced into.
> A war without orders."

Chapter 5 – Lines Between the Headlines

Karunapur, Suryadesh – January 17, 13:20 hrs

Suryadesh Independent News Bureau, Desk 5

Rishabh Kulkarni hadn't had lunch, sleep, or peace of mind since the story broke at dawn.

An "incident" near Point 427. No details. No visuals. No statements. Just whispers and the type of silence that made journalists feel like something huge was unfolding just behind a locked door.

And Rishabh hated locked doors.

He sat at Desk 5, the only one with two extra screens and a permanent coffee stain in the shape of the Suryadesh map. A fan above rotated in slow circles, doing nothing. The bureau was hot, loud, and slightly chaotic just the way he liked it.

On screen: border maps, live social media threads, and a SIA-flagged clip of **a funeral procession in Al-Bashir** claiming "Indian drone aggression." The footage was fake he was 90% sure. It reused visuals from a mudslide two years ago. But it had already gone viral.

His editor walked by, dropping a copy of the national daily on his desk.

"Page 3. Minister of Railways' dog gets state funeral. But no word from Defence."

Rishabh barely looked up. "That's because dogs don't leak classified intel."

The editor smirked and kept walking.

Rishabh opened his encrypted mail. One new message.

Subject: Do you want to know why Point 427 went dark?
Sender: Anonymous, via internal mail bounce

No attachments. Just a line of text in the body:

> "Check the train logs between Bhadravati and
> Akshepgarh. Car 6, Manifest 149-B.
> Not everyone on board was supposed to return."

Rishabh frowned.
It could've been a prank. But he recognised the phrasing. The cadence. It matched someone he'd once met while reporting on a military corruption scandal in Dandaka three years ago a clerk who had vanished a month later.

He checked the logs.

Train 2475 had passed Akshepgarh checkpoint hours before the listening post went dark. It was scheduled for a routine supplies drop to a forward unit but Car 6's manifest had **three unnamed entries**, with override codes normally reserved for defence contractors or intelligence assets.

He leaned back in his chair.

Who the hell was in that train car?

And why was someone leaking it to him?

His phone rang. A blocked number.

He answered on instinct. "Kulkarni."

A voice spoke. Distorted. Calm. Chillingly polite.

> "Mr. Kulkarni, you're a curious man. That makes you useful… or dead. Choose quickly."

Then it clicked off.

No trace.

Rishabh stared at the phone.

His hands were sweating, but his brain was sharper than ever.

He didn't know it yet but he had just stumbled into a corridor of secrets that connected:

- The silence at Point 427
- An unauthorised infiltration
- And the final doctrine waiting to be unsealed

And someone didn't want him just to tell the story.
They wanted him to walk into it.

Chapter 6 – Smoke Before Fire

Velinagar – January 17, 15:42 hrs

Portside Industrial Zone, Naval Dockyard Sector C

The explosion wasn't loud.

Not in the way bombs usually are not cinematic, not fireball-filling-the-sky. Just a sharp, clinical detonation, like someone had taken a scalpel to a beating artery and walked away before the blood sprayed.

A warehouse wall collapsed. Two bodies were thrown clear. A third was caught in the blast and vaporised identification would take hours, if possible. The fire was put out in twenty minutes. But the **real fire** had already started burning, unseen, in conference rooms across the capital.

Suryadesh Naval Command – 16:08 hrs

Vice Admiral Naresh Handa stared at the footage on the screen.

A delivery truck had parked at Dockyard Gate 3 exactly at 15:34 hrs. No badge scan. No log. The guard at the post was on a cigarette break four minutes off schedule. The truck didn't belong to any of the registered contractors.

By 15:42, it was ash and steel.

Three sailors injured. One civilian contractor presumed dead. A fuel line ruptured but mercifully didn't catch. No major structural damage. Yet every officer in the room looked like they were watching someone slowly sharpen a knife against their spine.

"This was a message," Handa muttered.

A naval intelligence officer nodded grimly. "Two minutes later and the blast would've hit the Barracuda-class engine holding bay."

"Coincidence?"

"I don't believe in those anymore, sir."

SIA (Surya Intelligence Agency) Internal Report – 16:20 hrs
Status: Preliminary Field Assessment
Classification: CODE ORANGE
Nature: Coordinated Low-Yield Detonation
Suspected Actor: Proxy Group with ties to Al-Bashir's internal militant network (Ummah-9)
Notes: Device was homemade, but trigger mechanism used advanced coding architecture possibly foreign supplied
Outcome: Infrastructure largely intact. Casualties limited. But message received.

Office of the National Security Advisor

Aarav Sen read the first intel burst in silence.

He'd expected something but not this. Not a public target. Not this calculated. Not this surgical.

He pressed a secure line.

"I want the port's entire personnel manifest screened. Anyone absent, unlogged, or off-pattern in the last 24 hours I want their names."

A pause. "What if it leads outside?"

"Then follow it."

"And if it leads inside?"

"Follow that harder."

He disconnected.

By now, word had reached the Prime Minister's in-flight communications team. A muted statement was drafted. "We condemn the attack." "We will not be provoked." "Investigations are underway."
The usual.

But Aarav knew better.

This wasn't provocation.

This was mapping. Probing. Testing.
A way to measure **how close Suryadesh was to reacting.**
How much blood they were willing to hold before it boiled.

Somewhere in the background, in a secure compound east of Bashirat, **Director Qadir Zameer** watched the same explosion on a private feed.

His assistant approached.

"Minimal damage. They'll call it terrorism. They'll absorb it."

Zameer smiled faintly. "That's the point. They must absorb this one."

He turned to another screen, this one marked "17:50 HRS" with coordinates flashing.

"Then we give them something they can't absorb."

Chapter 7 – Whispers in the Corridor

Karunapur, Suryadesh – January 17, 17:10 hrs

Surya Nagar Express (Train 2475) – Coach D7

Rishabh Kulkarni sat by the window, a backpack at his feet and a half-warmed samosa in his hand, trying not to look like a man being followed.

Because he was.

Somewhere in this train maybe in the coach behind him, maybe just one seat away someone was watching.

Ever since he published a vague tweet suggesting inconsistencies in military train logs, his inbox had gone silent. The tipster? Vanished. The link he received? Deactivated. And then, a call from an unlisted source, warning him not to travel by air.

So he took the train. Not for safety, but for **control.** Planes had check-ins and CCTV. Trains had doors, shadows, and toilets with two exits.

He unfolded the paper manifest he had printed in a rush.
Car 6. Manifest 149-B. Three unnamed passengers. No origin, no destination. Just "Official – Clear by Level 4."

He knew what that meant.

SIA or military intelligence.
Either way, they weren't supposed to be on that train.
And yet, all three were marked as disembarked before the blast at
Point 427.

> "Were they operatives?
> Or couriers?
> Or worse… ghosts?"

Rishabh scribbled the possibilities in a small notebook, the kind
only reporters and old spies still used. No cloud. No auto-save.
Just ink and paranoia.

The train slowed as it approached a mid-route junction.
He spotted a figure on the platform tall, bearded, wearing a
courier jacket in 32 degrees Celsius. He wasn't looking at the
train. He was looking through it.

Rishabh stood quickly and slipped into the passage between cars.

He paused by the restroom mirror, splashing water on his face.
His phone buzzed once.

New Message – Unsecured

"If you're reading this, they know you know. Trust no one. You
were never supposed to see the 427 file. Get to Surya Nagar. Drop
the notebook in a Redbox. Code 302."

The message vanished in three seconds.

Rishabh didn't even know what a **Redbox** was.

But he knew when a story was no longer a story.
It was a war zone with headlines.

Meanwhile, across the border…

Director Zameer stood at a sand-coloured compound, watching children run in a nearby field, laughter echoing as an imam's prayer finished in the distance.

An aide stepped close. "He's on the train. The journalist."

Zameer didn't look away. "Let him run. Let him think he's early."

The aide frowned. "Early?"

Zameer finally turned, his face unreadable.

"Because the real news… hasn't happened yet."

Chapter 8 – Between the Lines

Saphinia – January 17, 19:10 hrs

Hotel Marelle – Diplomatic Wing, Room 1704

Tara Mehta didn't bother closing the curtains.

The sky outside was deep cobalt, streaked with the golden glow of city lights bouncing off the glass skyline. A marble table held untouched fruit and two crystal tumblers only one had been used. She stood by the window in a black silk robe, loose at the waist, her bare leg visible through the slit. The room still carried the scent of her perfume jasmine and sandalwood with something else beneath it now: need.

She heard the soft knock. Once.

Her heart jumped. Not from fear but from something deeper. A mix of memory and muscle.

She opened the door.

He was there.

Anton Reznik. Older now. Salt at his temples. Grey coat. Scarf in hand. And that same presence an ex-diplomat who didn't play nice but made peace anyway.

Neither spoke. He closed the door behind him.

The moment it clicked shut, her breath hitched. His hands cupped her jaw, his mouth finding hers without ceremony. His kiss was firm, intentional, a man reclaiming what had never quite left him.

She responded in kind sliding her hands beneath his coat, feeling the tension in his back, the urgency he didn't try to hide.

But then he pulled back.

He looked at her.

"Are you still strong everywhere except where you need to be broken?"

She swallowed. "Yes."

He stepped closer. Voice low, gravelled.

"Then show me."

He tied the robe's sash around her wrists. Nothing harsh just enough. She let her arms rest at her sides, wrists bound, chest heaving. He made her walk to the window, the city below unaware of what power was doing above.

"Stand there," he said. "Back straight. Eyes down."

She obeyed.

Every command stripped something from her and it thrilled her. She, the Foreign Secretary of Suryadesh, the architect of half a dozen ceasefires, stood trembling in a hotel suite, heart thudding, nipples tight beneath silk, her thighs already slick with anticipation.

Anton untied the robe and let it fall.

He circled her slowly. Silent. Appreciative.

"You look like a goddess… begging to kneel."

She bit her lip.

He gripped her chin. "Say it."

"I want to kneel."

He sat on the edge of the bed. She dropped to her knees between his legs her wrists still bound, her eyes raised.

"What are you?"

She flushed, deeply.

"Yours."

He nodded.

He freed himself from his trousers and placed himself against her lips.

"Then prove it."

And she did.

With slow, wet, open-mouthed worship, she tasted him, her tongue working in practiced rhythm, moaning softly as he held her hair. His groans rumbled low in his chest, hands tightening around her head as he rocked into her mouth.

She looked up at him, eyes glazed, lips red and stretched, and he smiled.

"Still the best peacekeeper in the world."

Later, he took her to the bed.

Face down, wrists now tied to the headboard with her own robe. He took her from behind deep, hard, each thrust knocking breath from her lungs, her cries muffled in the pillow as her body quaked around him. No politics. No diplomacy. **Just ownership.**

And she loved it.

She came again and again until her throat was hoarse and her mind was empty.

Only then did he untie her.

She lay still, eyes closed, smiling through exhaustion.

"You'll go back tomorrow," he said, brushing her hair back. "And the world will kneel to you. But tonight…"

She finished for him.

"I needed to kneel."

Surya Nagar – January 17, 19:30 hrs

Private Residence – Sector 3B

He didn't know her real name.
To him, she was Leena. Early twenties. Laughter like rain, eyes like confession. She'd walked into his life in a bookstore with a smile and a question about poetry, and now she was in his bed.

He never suspected she was trained by Al-Bashir's elite spy unit. Or that her accent was an act.

She rode him slowly, lips parted, hands against his chest, moving with fluid sensuality. He moaned beneath her, lost in the feel of her tight warmth, the way she squeezed him with rhythm and precision.

"You like being used?" she whispered in his ear.

He nodded, dazed. "Yes."

She smiled sweetly. "Good."

She lowered her mouth to his bit his lip then picked up speed.

He came with a groan, hands gripping her hips. She let him finish. Let him believe it was real.

Then, as he lay there, catching his breath, she picked up his shirt and calmly tapped a bug into the collar lining.

He didn't even see it.

She kissed him once more.

"Next time," she whispered, "read me more poetry."

He chuckled.

And when she walked out of his apartment, she sent a single text to Zameer:

"Asset embedded. Voice and GPS active. Target believes he's in love."

Chapter 9 – The Final Straw

It was supposed to be a celebration.

The streets were choked with colour banners, rangoli, firecrackers. Children had sparklers. The air smelled of incense and sweets. A live band played patriotic songs in the town square. The mayor had just finished her speech.

Then the van exploded.

It blew the stage apart wood, metal, limbs, flags.

A second van swerved into the crowd. A man jumped out with a flamethrower.

He torched a line of food stalls, turning a dozen people into screaming silhouettes.

Then came the shooters.
Twelve men in groups of three, armed with assault rifles and suicide belts.

They didn't shout slogans.
They didn't wear insignia.
They just started **killing.**

08:01 hrs

At the maternity clinic 300 meters away, two men walked in calmly, guns hidden in flower baskets.

They detonated in the waiting room.

Twenty-four dead. Twelve of them women in labor.

08:04 hrs – Drone Footage, SIA Field Command
Casualties Visible: 100+
Active Hostiles: 3 units still mobile
Emergency Response: Local police overwhelmed

08:06 hrs – Primary School, Sector 9B
Another van exploded outside the school gate where children had gathered for the post-festival song performance.

The shockwave shattered the windows. Shrapnel tore into children's faces, torsos, necks. A girl named Myra was thrown six feet into a wall. She was nine.

Inside, two men with machetes stormed in.
No guns. No bombs.
Just blades.

They started hacking. Quietly. Room by room.

A teacher who shielded five children bled to death behind a desk.
A boy who tried to run had his legs taken off.

08:12 hrs – Train Station
The 07:45 express had just pulled in. Two terrorists moved along the platform with automatic shotguns. They didn't reload. They just dropped the spent guns and pulled out knives.

By the time they were shot dead, **forty-seven people were already down.**
Dead. Dying. Screaming.

A toddler was found hugging the leg of his father's severed body.

08:15 hrs – National TV Feed (Intercepted by SIA)

A masked man appeared.

> "You wanted peace? You taught your people not to fight?

> Look at your women burn.
> Look at your gods fall.

> You deserve this. You sleep, while your blood boils."

Then he shot a woman in the head. On live feed.

By 08:22 hrs – the death toll crossed 180.
By 08:30 – **212.**
By 08:45 – **263.**

Among them:

- 37 children
- 5 doctors
- 4 police officers
- 2 pregnant women
- 1 newborn

SIA Crisis Command – 08:48 hrs

Aarav Sen's voice cut through the silence.

"Send the directive. Tag every known Ummah-9 location.
Mark cross-border escape routes for airstrike clearance.
Confirm blackout protocol.
This… is war."

Prime Minister Aditya Rao – 08:51 hrs – aboard return flight

He watched the drone footage.

A girl with half a face crawled toward a barricade.

Her mother lay behind her still, arms stretched out like she was trying to pull her child into death with her.

Aditya closed his eyes.

"Draft the address. No more restraint.

We will speak peace no longer."

**Military Command Authorisation: OPERATION GARUDA –
PENDING FINAL CODE**

Timer: 04:00 hrs
Strike Radius: 9 confirmed cross-border targets
Launch Type: Aerial, ground, and cyber coordinated response
Doctrine Level: RED

The final straw had broken not just the camel's back

It shattered the whole cart.

And what came next…
Would not be diplomacy.

Chapter 10 – The Other Side of Smoke

Bashirat, Al-Bashir – January 17, 22:40 hrs onward
Private Compound – North Ridge Safe Zone

In the west wing of the villa, behind curtains thick enough to muffle the music, **the real celebration** had begun.

A line of young women, dressed in silk veils and anklets, danced in a low-lit room filled with velvet cushions and drug smoke. None were older than twenty. Some younger. Some terrified.

They danced for commanders. For politicians. For killers. And those men watched with legs spread, hands full, smiles dripping with power.

Rashid sat with a girl on each knee, neither of whom spoke the local language. One fed him wine from a jewelled goblet, the other slid her fingers slowly down his chest. She giggled on command.

He grabbed her wrist mid-stroke and pulled her into his lap his fingers sliding up her thigh beneath the silk. "Tell me how I saved your faith," he whispered in her ear.

She didn't understand the words.
But she nodded anyway.

Further down the hall, a room reeked of sweat and perfume.

Three senior militia officers passed a bottle of Jinzhou scotch between them while two women stripped to bare skin lay blindfolded on a low mattress, waiting for instructions. A third woman knelt between one man's legs, moving slowly, rhythmically, as he smoked a cigar and stared at the muted television on the wall.

It showed fire in Akshepgarh.

"Still burning," he muttered with a smile.

Another room had turned into a private opium den.
A General lay back on silk cushions while a woman, high and shirtless, danced on his chest, arms swaying like vines.

"Bring more girls," he barked. "And fewer tears this time."

In the courtyard, under the stars, two young boys from the local madrassa were being led by older men in military jackets. The men laughed. The boys didn't.

From the upper balcony, **Director Qadir Zameer** watched this depravity unfold every room, every shadow, every bare back and empty eye.

He had seen war before.

But what he had created here tonight was worse. It was not war.

It was **victory without conscience.**

He crushed out his cigarette, turned, and walked inside.

The music played on.

Chapter 11 – Ashes and Flags

Surya Nagar, Suryadesh – January 18, 09:00 hrs
National Day of Mourning

The first responders didn't cry.

Not yet.

They moved like machines fast, coordinated, numbed by the scale of what they were seeing. **Firetrucks** pumped into buildings that no longer stood. **Ambulances** pulled out bodies with no names. **Paramedics** screamed for supplies while they knelt in blood.

But none of it was enough.

Not for the old man still cradling his granddaughter's charred hand.
Not for the woman who had lost both sons and stood, barefoot and screaming, in the ashes of her street.
Not for the schoolteacher who vomited after finding her student's body torn in half behind the playground gate.

And not for the volunteer whose job was to **scrape flesh from concrete.**

He tried. For hours. With gloves and rags and all the strength in his arms. But the blood had cooked into the pavement. It wouldn't come off.

So he dropped to his knees and sobbed.

And beside him, another young man poured water from a bottle over the stained street. "At least wash it," he whispered, "before the mothers come."

Every hospital in the northern zone overflowed.
Children with burns. Women with torn lungs.
Dozens who couldn't be saved, lined under white sheets, tagged only by wristbands and hope.

A nurse screamed when she unzipped one body bag and saw her cousin.
A fireman refused to leave the scene after his wife was brought in, her hair still braided for the festival, half her face gone.

By 07:00 hrs, the government declared a National Day of Mourning.

But the people didn't wait for a decree.

They were already gathering.

By 08:00 hrs – Surya Nagar Civic Grounds

A sea of people had formed thousands dressed in white. Some with photos. Some with folded hands. Some with eyes red from crying all night.

Drums beat slowly.
Not for celebration. But for grief.
And **justice.**

On the main dais, **264 coffins** were laid in rows.
Each draped in the national flag.
Each identical in shape, but not in story.

One held a newborn.
One held only a girl's schoolbag, because there was no body to find.

A mother clutched that bag like it had a heartbeat.
A father beat his chest until his hands broke open.

The Prime Minister had not arrived.

The military had not spoken.

The people whispered:

> "They have never hit back hard."

> "We grieve. They talk."

> "When will they burn for what they've done to us?"

09:00 hrs – Silence

A single drumbeat.
Then another.

Then the weeping began.

From the stage, a child survivor was helped forward.
She was ten. Wrapped in gauze. Face half-bandaged.
She held the flag that had covered her brother's body.

She said only one word.

"Why?"

And the crowd exploded into tears.

Not because they had no answer.
But because they all did.

Across Suryadesh –

Schools stood silent.
Markets shuttered.
News anchors wore black.
Temples held prayer vigils.

And everywhere, one question echoed beneath it all:

"Will we retaliate this time? Or mourn again?"

Inside the National Security Secretariat, **Aarav Sen** stood at a window watching the procession on a silent screen.

His hand was clenched.

"Enough," he whispered.

Chapter 12 – Quiet Before Thunder

Suryadesh – January 18, 19:00 hrs

National Broadcast Room, Surya Nagar – 19:00 hrs

Aditya Rao adjusted the collar of his black bandhgala. It was too tight. Or maybe he was.

The room was still. Technicians whispered. The countdown began.

Five. Four. Three. Two

The red light blinked on.

He looked into the camera not as a leader. As a man carrying the weight of **264 dead**, most of them children.

"We are not at war.

But yesterday, they declared one on us.

We pleaded for peace.
They answered with fire."

His hand trembled once. He folded it into a fist behind the podium.

"We will respond. But not with fury.
With **resolve**.

And we will do it together as a nation.

Not fractured by politics.

United by pain."

He stepped away from the podium, breath held for three full seconds before the anthem rolled.

Below Surya Nagar – 19:00 hrs

SIA Operations Subnet, Black Level

Aarav Sen pressed his palm to the scanner. The door unlocked with a hydraulic hiss.

Inside: low-lit consoles, humming machines, and three handpicked officers all off the books.

He opened a titanium case.

"Operation Garuda – Emergency Activation Protocols"

Three targets were already locked:
- **Camp Siraj** – weapons and insurgent manpower

- **Relay Base Anwar** – Al-Bashir's underground comm grid
- **Compound 17** – the villa where they had partied after the massacre

He picked up the red-line phone.

"Shadow Group. Status?"

"Airborne. Seventeen minutes from border. Holding pattern. Standing by."

He stared at the screen. A map showed three flight groups in formation, silent and armed.

No one knew.

Not the Defence Ministry.
Not the Joint Chiefs.
Not even the Prime Minister.

"You'll have your answer before you cross," Aarav said.

"If you don't, return. Do not fire without my word."

He ended the call.

He didn't blink.

Prime Minister's Jet – 19:25 hrs

Aditya sat alone in the cabin, coat off, tie loosened, a folder of casualties in front of him. He didn't read the names. He couldn't.

His mind raced.

> Who would oppose it? Who would stall? What if they reject it again? What if this becomes another compromise?

His aide appeared. "Cabinet and opposition leaders are ready. All waiting in Chamber One."

Aditya nodded, knuckles white around the folder.

Cabinet Chamber – 19:52 hrs

The room was full. Suits. Stars. Silence.

Aditya stood at the head of the long mahogany table, lit like a courtroom.

> "We are not here to mourn. We've done that.

> We are here to respond.

> I want to invoke wartime command protocols, brief the armed forces for retaliatory air strikes, and transfer temporary operational control to the military."

The silence broke.

And turned into noise.

"Not without Parliament."
"It will collapse our diplomatic stance."
"We can't act without consensus."
"The UN will condemn this."
"Jinzhou will retaliate economically."
"We need a panel first."
"We need Geneva."
"We need time."

Aditya closed his eyes. For a moment, he was no longer the Prime Minister.

He was just a father. Of a seven-year-old boy.

And the bag of one such child was still lying unclaimed in a hospital in Akshepgarh contents melted to the lining. Crayons. A picture of a flag. A lunchbox.

He opened his eyes.

"They danced while we buried our dead.

We have done nothing but wait.

And you still want to talk?"

20:44 hrs – SIA Subnet

Aarav stood watching a muted feed of the Cabinet chamber. No sound, just faces angry, sweating, posturing.

He tapped a button.

> "Shadow Group. Five minutes to Checkpoint Delta. Maintain radio silence until direct confirmation."

"Copy."

He walked to the side console, activated a burner relay.

> "If he doesn't get it…
> we do."

Prime Minister's Office – 21:15 hrs

The room had thinned. Voices had quieted. The Leader of Opposition now stood.

> "We've disagreed many times.

> But this… this massacre? We cannot stand behind closed lips.

> You have our support."

Others stood. One by one.

Not everyone. But **enough**.

The Defence Minister nodded gravely.

"We're ready."

Aditya turned slowly to the only man still seated in silence.

"Aarav. Inform the Air Command.

The country has spoken."

Aarav looked up, nodded once.

"Understood."

He stepped out of the room without urgency.

Then into a secure room.

And picked up the red phone.

"Proceed. Full release.

Strike authorised."

Chapter 13 – When Fire Falls

January 18, 22:12 hrs – Suryadesh Time / 21:42 hrs – Al-Bashir Local

In the Skies Above the Border

The cockpit glowed cold green, HUD blinking altitude, range, payload locks.

Squadron Leader Dev Mehra gripped the stick lightly. Below him: nothing but darkness. Above him: two wingmen. Behind him: history waiting to be written.

> "This is Shadow One to all birds. Marking final approach. Confirm nav. All systems green."

Three voices echoed in: calm, precise.

> "Weapons armed."
> "Target visuals confirmed."
> "Standing by."

Dev's screen flashed. Border lock.
A pause.

Then one word from Command:

> "Proceed."

He lowered his altitude by 200 meters, breaking cloud.

And saw it.

The first target **Camp Siraj** lay beneath him like a dimly lit
anthill: barracks, fuel depots, trucks. He could see movement.
Heat signatures men walking. Smoking. Laughing. Unaware.

"Shadow One to Lead initiating strike pattern. Fox One."

He pressed the trigger.

Two missiles detached with a scream.
Followed by four more from the flanking jets.

In four seconds, **Camp Siraj was no longer on the map.**

Fuel tanks ruptured. Barracks crumpled. The fireball swallowed
ten men whole.

Their screams didn't reach the cockpit.

Al-Bashir, Near Relay Base Anwar – 21:46 hrs

Teenagers in sandals ran when the first boom hit.

They didn't understand. It wasn't a drone. It wasn't insurgents
firing AKs. **This was something else.**

Something from above.

Missiles tore through the relay tower's upper grid. Power lines whipped through the air like metal serpents. Flames shot out from the underground bunker as signals died across three sectors.

The blackout spread across half a province.

The fire did more.

Bashirat Outskirts – Compound 17 (Target 3)

Director Qadir Zameer's Private Holding

He was halfway through a classified briefing when the walls shook.

Windows shattered. Ceiling tiles rained down. The chandelier above snapped from its hinges and crashed onto the marble.

His ears rang as he hit the floor.

Bodyguards rushed in. Guns drawn. One dragged him by the collar.

"Sir! Sir! They hit the compound!"

"No… No, they wouldn't "

He was cut off by the second strike.
It didn't hit the villa.

It hit the **adjacent guesthouse**, where his **nephew** a promising intel officer and two visiting cousins had been staying.

The building vanished in a white flash.

When the smoke cleared, it wasn't there anymore.

Just ash. Shattered stone. And parts of a red scarf.

Zameer stood slowly. Dust covering his face. His lip cut. His mind slow to catch up.

"They knew," he said aloud. "They knew exactly where to strike."

He turned to his aide.

> "Get me every camera. Every channel. Every listening post.
>
> I want to know who sold me out."

Surya Nagar – Prime Minister's Private Briefing Room – 22:14 hrs

Aditya stared at the live telemetry report that had just landed in his aide's hand. The aide looked confused. Then horrified.

"Sir... they're already inside Al-Bashir.

Shadow Group launched. All three targets engaged."

Aditya's eyes widened.

He looked at Aarav, who stood at the far end of the room, silent.

"You... You sent them."

Aarav didn't flinch.

"I waited. You asked for the mandate. I gave them a holding order.

But yes. They're in the sky.

And they were never coming back without fire."

The room fell silent. Ministers stared. Some in awe. Some in fury.

Aditya turned to them. Took a breath. His voice even.

"Gentlemen.

The first wave has struck.

Operation Garuda is underway."

No one spoke.

Because **war had already begun.**

Chapter 14 – Ripples Through Glass

January 19, 01:10 hrs IST

Surya Nagar, Prime Minister's Crisis Chamber

The room buzzed. Foreign Affairs. Intelligence. Army brass. Communications.

Aditya Rao sat with a fresh file in hand. **Damage assessments** from the Garuda strike:

- **112 enemy combatants confirmed killed.**
- Two key bunkers vaporised.
- Zameer's private compound "critically impacted."
- Civilian casualties: **unknown.**

The **international line-board** blinked with red alerts.

US State Department – urgent inquiry.
European Commission – emergency session called.
Redvale Bloc – condemnation pending.
UN SecGen – requesting explanation.
Jinzhou – "monitoring situation with grave concern."

The room was hot with urgency.

"Sir, should we accept the UN statement?"

"No."

"Call back Redvale?"

"No."

"What about?"

Aditya stood.

"Get me live press coverage. Tonight. I will speak for this nation
before the world puts words in our mouth."

The room froze.

Bashirat, Al-Bashir – Director Zameer's Underground Command Bunker

The remains of his nephew were sealed in a steel coffin. DNA
confirmed. No body to dress. Just shards.

Zameer stared at the monitor.
His satellite link with eastern assets had gone dark.
His logistics officer was dead.
His party had become a pyre.

Still, he didn't blink.

"We underestimated them."

He turned to his surviving commanders.

"That won't happen again."

A map rolled open.

"We activate all northern units. Counter-intel teams. Let the NGOs cry about civilian zones every inch of them is a shelter for informants.

We hit their faith. Their civilians. Their cameras. Let them drown in reaction."

He lit a cigarette, the scar on his cheek from the blast still raw.

"If it's war they want

we'll show them what kind of war we're built for."

New York, London, Geneva, Beijing – 04:00 to 07:00 Local Time

International media screamed headlines:
- **"Suryadesh Strikes First: Air Raid Over Al-Bashir"**
- **"Unilateral Action or Justified Retaliation?"**
- **"Nuclear Powers on Collision Path"**
- **"Zameer Compound Hit – Al-Bashir Intelligence Chief Targeted"**

In every embassy in Suryadesh, lights stayed on.
Journalists hammered press officers. Protesters gathered outside
consulates. Diplomats requested urgent debriefings.

In one chamber in Geneva, a UN delegate whispered:

> "If this isn't stopped now, we'll be watching a border war
> explode into a global shift."

Surya Nagar, 04:55 hrs

Aditya stood in his private office. Alone.

He watched replays of the strike footage. Watched the explosion
at Compound 17 again.

He didn't speak.

Not until the aide walked in.

> "Sir, you'll be live in 12 minutes."

Aditya turned.

> "Then let's make it very clear to the world

> We didn't start this war.

> But we will finish it."

Chapter 15 – The Counter-fire

January 19, 05:55 hrs IST

Sector 9, Suryadesh Northern Defence Grid – 05:55 hrs

Radar stations lit up like a festival gone wrong.

"Multiple objects inbound."
"Speeds match loiter drones. Ten-plus confirmed. Two larger possibly cruise."
"Heading toward Vajra Base and Sector 5 CivGrid."

The air defence chief didn't hesitate.

"Scramble interceptors. Activate surface batteries. Launch grid intercept now."

Within ninety seconds, the sky above Vajra exploded in brilliance.

Six surface-to-air missiles screamed into the stratosphere.
Anti-air drones launched from silos.
Two manned interceptors banked hard and climbed fast.

On the ground, sirens screamed.

Intercepted.
Neutralised.

No impact.

The base commander exhaled.

"So this is how they answer."

Suryadesh Interior – 06:22 hrs

City of Nalgad, Metro Rail Station

The guard noticed the man in the green kurta just a second too late.

He wasn't carrying anything. No bags. No backpack.
Just a pressurised detonator belt under his tunic and a remote in his left hand.

Boom.

The blast ripped through three compartments of the early morning train.

Steel twisted. Glass exploded. People screamed. Others simply vanished.

Twenty-two dead.
Dozens more bleeding on the platform.

Before the dust cleared, two more men in the station **opened fire.**

They didn't run. They weren't there to survive.

They wanted **fear** to spread faster than their bullets.

Surya Nagar, SIA Crisis Response – 06:50 hrs

Aarav stood over the incident report, his jaw set.

> "Three sleeper cells activated. One in Nalgad. One near
> Sudhpur Mall. Another tried to breach the Defence
> Housing Block but was intercepted."

His aide added grimly, "They're using a mix of local
sympathisers and foreign handlers. The man in Nalgad came in as
a cultural student last year."

> "He came to study music," Aarav muttered. "And left with
> shrapnel."

Bashirat – 04:35 hrs Local Time

Zameer lit a cigarette with shaking fingers.

But his voice was calm.

> "We lost the skies.
> So now we take their streets."

He turned to his deputy.

"Start a blackout campaign. Cyber-ops. Disinformation. Target their opposition parties. Leak their war plans. Make it look like a grab for power."

He stepped into his war room.

"While they defend bombs, we make them question their own house."

International Media – 07:45 hrs IST
- **"Suryadesh Struck First – UN Panel Divided"**
- **"Reckless Escalation or Righteous Response?"**
- **"Intelligence Chief Aarav Sen Wields Unauthorised Power?"**
- **"Aditya Rao's Cabinet Under Fire – Did the Strike Break Protocol?"**

Three major embassies called for "restraint."
One recalled its ambassador for "consultation."
Two of Suryadesh's trade partners froze arms supply discussions.

In Geneva, the representative from Jinzhou pushed a statement:

"Let us not forget: escalation benefits those who hide the truth.

Mediation, not missiles, is the language of civilisation."

Aditya read the casualty report. Then the economic forecast. Then the security bulletin.

"How bad is it?" he asked.

Aarav responded.

"Terror cells are activated. They hit three targets. Air defence stopped the missiles but they've gone asymmetric now.

And the world? They're not with us. Not fully."

Aditya looked around the room.

His eyes burned.
"They want to make us doubt ourselves.

They want us to slow down.

So now… we don't."

He turned to the Defence Minister.

"Prepare the second wave.

This time, we hit them where it hurts the most."

Chapter 16 – The Second Wave

January 19, 13:15 hrs IST

Surya Nagar – Prime Minister's War Room

The room was locked. No aides. No phones. Just Aditya Rao, Aarav Sen, the Defence Minister, three military chiefs, and a map glowing red over the central table.

"We hit infrastructure, communications, and a symbolic target," Aarav said, voice crisp. "Now we go deeper. Strategic dismantling."

He marked three circles on the map:

1. **Khalif Bazaar Stock Exchange, Bashirat** – the economic lifeline.

2. **State Broadcast HQ** – the propaganda engine feeding hate.

3. **Al-Tayir Command Citadel** – an abandoned palace turned covert coordination hub.

The Defence Minister leaned in.

"We can't just drop bombs. Civilians surround the Exchange. And the Citadel's shielded."

Aarav nodded.

"That's why this time, we use **people**."

13:30 hrs – Blackout Unit Bravo – Southern Suryadesh Airstrip

Six men and two women in desert-grade combat gear loaded into a stealth-modified transport. No names. No ranks. Just call signs.

Inside their briefing capsule:
- **Cut comms and backup fuel lines to the stock exchange.**
- **Hijack the State Broadcast feed and stream a pre-loaded video of Al-Bashir's atrocities.**
- **Mark the Citadel for an airstrike once internal resistance confirms exfil.**

"In. Quiet. Fast. Out. Light the match for a nation to see," said the team leader.

One soldier kissed a dog tag. Another prayed.
Then they were airborne.

Meanwhile – Bashirat, Al-Bashir

Social media exploded.

#BashiratBleeds
#SuryadeshStrikesInnocents
#HumanRightsOrHorror

Dozens of graphic posts showed women weeping, a hospital façade cracked by shrapnel, a child's face dust-covered in a school corridor.

Except…

The footage was three years old. The women were **paid**, the child **alive and well in a refugee camp** outside Al-Bashir.

It didn't matter.

> "Suryadesh is burning our mosques."
> "My sister died in a bakery airstrike."
> "They dropped white phosphorus."
> "Peace! Not genocide!"

The tweets trended globally.

In Suryadesh, a **handful of verified influencers** began to post:

> "Do we really know the truth?"
> "Maybe we provoked this?"
> "Our govt needs to stop this war before we become monsters."

All of them **quietly funded** through shell companies traced to Redvale and Al-Bashir.

SIA Counterintel Hub – 14:18 hrs

Aarav paced.

> "Track all IP routes. Start pulling digital audits on
> influencers. If we don't win the algorithm war, we lose
> control of our own people."

His aide reported, "Two verified handles just posted 'Aditya is
committing war crimes.' Tags are already crossing 300K shares."

> "Then flood them with truth.
> Leak every image from Compound 17.
> Show the corpses. Show their parties."

Bashirat – 14:55 hrs Local Time

Elite Team Insertion

The blackout team touched down two miles from the Khalif
Bazaar financial ring. Silent gliders. Ground camo. Pre-dawn
cover.

Phase 1: Two operators severed the underground fibre lines,
while a third rewired the grid to reroute into SIA-controlled
receivers.

Phase 2: A female operative climbed the transmission tower of
State Broadcast HQ. At 15:10 local time, she plugged in a

payload that killed every Al-Bashir broadcast channel and replaced it with a **live feed** from Akshepgarh's aftermath.

Millions watched, horrified, as reality punctured the lie.

Children crying. Blood-soaked temples. Flames.

Al-Tayir Citadel – 15:24 hrs

Three SIA saboteurs disguised as clerks made their way to the lower chambers. One placed a beacon on the main corridor vault. Another slipped a signal booster into the main comm terminal.

At 15:32, the extraction signal went green.

Vajra Base – 15:35 hrs IST

A command pilot received one order:

"Citadel is lit. Target confirmed. Strike window is ninety seconds."

"Copy. Fox Three."

Two hypersonic missiles dropped from the sky like **the judgment of history**.

The Citadel exploded in three roaring pulses.

Director Zameer stood in a conference with military planners.

An aide burst in.

"Sir… the Exchange is cut. Broadcast HQ is down.

And the Citadel "

The wall behind them shook.

The lights cut out.

Dust rained from the ceiling.

Zameer's ears rang.

A commander lay on the floor eyes wide, neck twisted.

A portrait of Al-Bashir's founding general split down the middle.

Zameer stood still for a moment.

"This isn't war.

This is demolition."

Chapter 17 – Ghosts in the Feed

January 19, 19:10 hrs IST

Surya Nagar, Central Plaza – 19:10 hrs

A man held up a sign.
It read: **"We do not want apologies. We want victory."**

Beside him, a woman burned a paper dove.
Children beat steel plates with sticks echoes of protest
reengineered into a **war cry**.

Across Suryadesh, the nation was no longer holding its breath.
It was **breathing fire**.

Social Media – 19:30 hrs

What had begun as outrage had hardened into clarity.

After the blackout team's upload of the real massacre footage
unedited, brutal, undeniable **even international feeds shifted**.

"Akshepgarh was genocide."
"They danced after killing children."
"No more questions. Only answers."

The SIA's digital team flooded the feeds with raw testimonials:
 - A mother holding a melted lunchbox.

• A paramedic who had lost both hands trying to pull a body from fire.

• A ten-year-old who couldn't speak, only sign the shape of her sister's face.

Hashtags that once read #Restraint were now replaced with:

#AshForAsh
#WarWithoutMercy
#OperationGarudaForever

Public Sentiment Polls – Internal Ministry Feed

• 87% supported continued strikes.

• 74% wanted **no negotiation**.

• 63% said Aditya Rao had "waited too long."

• 92% said they trusted **Aarav Sen** more than the Parliament.

The people had chosen.

Not peace.
Not politics.
Just **vengeance**.

Bashirat – Al-Bashir Military Cemetery – 18:55 hrs Local Time

Zameer stood alone.

The crater from the Citadel strike still smouldered across the hill.
But he wasn't looking at it.

He was looking at a **headstone**, barely standing.

It read: **"Kamran Qadir. Son. Officer. Dreamer."**

His nephew. Dead. Burned. Identified only by blood samples and
a melted dog tag.

Zameer didn't cry.

He pulled out a folded piece of paper crumpled, soiled.

It was a **child's drawing** Kamran had once made, years ago, of
"Baba's big office."

Zameer set it on the grave.
Then lit it with a match.

It curled, blackened, and disappeared.

His aide approached.

> "Sir, a high-value Suryadesh minister is travelling to
> Malwa Province next week. Minimal security.
>
> It can be made to look like tribal unrest."

Zameer didn't look at him.

"No."

A pause.

"No distractions. No confusion. No deniability."

He turned slowly.

"We strike one. But we make it personal.

Something **Aditya Rao will never recover from**."

His eyes gleamed not with madness, but **calculation**.

"I will make the people who follow him… afraid to love again."

Chapter 18 – The Rift

January 20, 07:20 hrs IST

Prime Minister's Residence, Surya Nagar

The room was quiet.

No aides. No generals. No advisors. Just two men.

Prime Minister **Aditya Rao**, dressed in a rumpled kurta he hadn't changed since the night before.
And **Aarav Sen**, still in his black Nehru jacket, the collar pressed tight like a sealed truth.

Aditya poured two cups of tea but only placed one on the table.

He took his seat across from the man who, by all legal accounts, had committed **mutiny without punishment.**

"You disobeyed me," Aditya said calmly.

Aarav didn't answer.

"You launched a strike. Not just a warning shot.
Three high-value targets, without clearance.

You told no one. Not even me."

"I waited," Aarav said. "Then I acted."

Aditya's fist tightened on the armrest.

"You made me a spectator in my own government."

"No," Aarav said, evenly. "I made you a survivor."

Silence.

Outside, protestors gathered again. This time not in anger but in
vigil. Holding flags. Pictures of the dead.
Chanting **his** name. Aarav's.
Aditya looked down at the tea, then back up.

"You didn't just go around the system, Aarav.
You killed it.

What happens when this war ends? Do we hand the
country over to unelected ghosts with clearance codes and
satellite uplinks?"

Aarav leaned forward.

"You think we still have a 'when.'
I'm telling you: we only have '**if**.'"

"You've changed," Aditya said softly.

"You haven't," Aarav replied.

That landed. Hard.

Aditya stood and walked to the window. The rising sun painted the city in ash-gold light. A bird circled, then vanished.

"They want war now," Aditya said. "Not just the government. The people.
But we both know war is like acid.
It burns what it touches, even if you win."

Aarav's voice hardened.

"Then stop sending children into fire and calling it restraint."

A pause.

"I never wanted this," Aditya said.

"Neither did I," Aarav replied. "But **I prepared for it**.
And I won't apologise for keeping us alive."

Aditya turned, furious.

"No! You didn't keep us alive. You just delayed something worse.
Zameer isn't beaten. He's angry. And you just made it personal."

"It was always personal," Aarav snapped.
"We were the only ones pretending it
wasn't."

Silence again. This time heavier.

Aditya picked up the untouched cup of tea and set it beside Aarav.

"One more strike, Aarav…
And you don't do it without my voice in your ear."

Aarav looked at the cup. Then at Aditya.

"Then speak loud enough. Because the next time… we might not
get to whisper."

Chapter 19 – The Bait

January 22, 11:42 hrs IST
Multiple Locations, Suryadesh

It began with **a missed call**.

Then a second.

Then three bombs within seven minutes.

SIA Convoy Route – Eastern Belt Highway, 11:42 hrs

Aarav Sen sat in the backseat of the armoured vehicle, reading a field report on Zameer's family movements his daughter had vanished from Bashirat two nights ago. Possibly a decoy. Possibly something worse.

The SUV ahead exploded mid-turn.

His driver swerved instinctively.
Wrong move.

A second blast ripped through the roadside, flipping their vehicle into the divider.

Dazed, bleeding, Aarav kicked open the door, half-crawled out, gun drawn.

Bullets cracked from a motorbike speeding past.
Aarav fired once hit the gunman square in the chest.

Two more shooters emerged from a parked garbage truck.

Aarav ducked, aimed, fired.

One kill.
One wounded.
One bolt of agony through his shoulder.

But he lived.

Barely.

South Command Office, Surya Nagar – 11:45 hrs

Defence Minister **Anil Rane** exited the elevator.

As he approached the lobby, a man in a courier uniform approached.

No words.

Just a detonator.

Security tackled him at the last second. The blast tore through the far end of the glass atrium.

Shrapnel flew. One guard lost an eye.

Rane survived by twelve feet and a stroke of timing.

Prime Minister's Residence – 11:48 hrs

Aditya Rao had just finished a call with the French ambassador.

His son, **Ishaan**, had taken his tutor to the garden for chess. The boy loved chess. Aditya smiled when he saw them from the window.

Then his phone rang again his wife.

"There's something happening. I heard "

The sound of gunfire cracked through the compound.

Screams. Guards running. A burst of automatic fire.

Aditya dropped the phone.

Ran.

He reached the garden just as two operatives in stolen security uniforms fell under bullets from the PM's Special Guard.

It was over in twelve seconds.

But **one body didn't move.**

The tutor.

Shot twice in the back.
Died shielding Ishaan with her own body.

She had worked with the family for four years. Taught Ishaan
math. Spoke Hindi with a Tamil accent. Made the boy laugh.
Her name was **Revathi Iyer.**

And she was gone.

Crisis Chamber – 13:10 hrs

The room was silent.

Aditya stood at the head of the table, shaking.

"Three attempts. One message."

Aarav, arm bandaged, eyes steely, said nothing.

Aditya continued.

"They didn't go after strategy. They went after **faces**.

Me.
Rane.
You."

A pause.

"But they killed someone who didn't even carry a title."

His voice cracked. Not from weakness but fury.

"Enough silence. We strike.

I want Zameer's **entire circle** erased."

Aarav met his gaze.

"Then I need **full control**.

No press briefings. No debates.

Just a shadow war. For every ghost they gave us we give them ruin."

Aditya didn't hesitate.

"Do it."

Meanwhile – Bashirat, Al-Bashir – 13:42 hrs Local Time

Zameer poured himself a drink.

His aide entered.

"Failed to kill Sen. Rao unharmed. Tutor dead. Child survived."

Zameer raised his glass.

"A child who learns what war is by watching the person who protected him die…

That child will grow up afraid.

We've already won the next battle."

Chapter 20 – Shadowfront

January 23, 01:10 hrs IST

Surya Nagar, SIA Strategic Command – Black Level 6

The lights were dim.
Not for mood. For focus.

Aarav Sen stood in front of a screen displaying a living map of **Al-Bashir's arteries**:
Airbases. Naval ports. Fuel lines. Intelligence hubs. Trade corridors.
Each marked not with red
But **with blinking white lights**. Targets. Alive. Movable.
Precious.

He looked at the six operatives seated before him.

> "We do not hit children.
> We do not bomb cities.
>
> We kill the beating heart of a failed state…
> and let the body rot on its own."

The plan was simple.

"Collapse the lie.
Cripple the wallet.
Cut off the arms.

And make the world forget it ever believed them."

Bashirat Stock Commission – 03:44 hrs Local Time

Three men in suits left a meeting with Al-Bashir's top economic minister.

They didn't see the fourth man behind the tinted cab.

One suppressed shot.
One decapitated network.

That minister had been secretly laundering oil transit revenue through a Redvale shell fund linked to chemical weapons procurement.

Now?
He was a body in a storm drain.

Naval Base El-Qadir – 05:15 hrs

Two stealth jets from Suryadesh's southern wing crossed radar undetected.

They fired **hyper-glide payloads** onto docked warships loaded for a planned regional naval exercise.

Four ships were reduced to burning steel.
The command tower was flattened.

The sea caught fire.

The drills were canceled.
The message, clear.

Zurich, Private Embassy Meeting Room – 06:02 hrs CET

A top diplomat from Al-Bashir received a brown envelope.

Inside:

- Copies of his offshore account transactions.
- Satellite images of him at a Redvale-owned club.
- Audio of a conversation about oil-for-missiles arrangements.
- A note:

"Withdraw support for Al-Bashir or this goes public."

Within twelve hours, **Redvale abstained from a UN resolution condemning Suryadesh.**

Al-Bashir Intelligence Directorate – 07:40 hrs Local Time

A pre-dawn explosion destroyed the western surveillance wing of Zameer's intelligence compound.

Inside were servers.
Encrypted footage.
And the surveillance files of every Suryadesh asset they had turned or tried to.

All gone.

Zameer was not in the building.
But he felt the flames from his office rooftop.

He said nothing.
He poured a drink.
And watched the smoke rise.

UN Headquarters, Geneva – 10:15 hrs GMT

Documents were leaked to the press.

Not by SIA operatives.
By their proxies.

Details showed Al-Bashir's secret camps.
Execution logs.
Video clips of fake "massacres" staged for international pity.

Headlines shifted.

"Al-Bashir Played Us All?"
"New Dossier Reveals War Crimes Behind Closed Borders"
"Zameer's Lie Machine Unravels"

In just a day, the narrative had turned.

Surya Nagar, Prime Minister's Residence – 14:00 hrs

Aditya sat with Aarav in silence.

The list of completed operations was in his hand.

"Naval base gone.
Intelligence wing crippled.
Trade envoy blackmailed.
Stock minister executed.
Global media flipped."

He looked up.

"You didn't touch his family."

Aarav nodded.

"That was never the mission."

Aditya leaned back.

"What is?"

Aarav answered softly.

"That when he's finally alone…

He hears nothing.

No phones.
No allies.
No economy.

Just silence. And the sound of his own failure."

Bashirat – 18:30 hrs Local Time

Zameer sat at his desk.

Reports in flames.

Allies withdrawing.

Three ships gone.
One trade pact collapsed.
His daughter the only family he had left under protection outside the country.

He poured his last bottle of 30-year-old whiskey into a tea glass.
Drank it slowly.

Then whispered:

> "So this is how a nation dies.
> Not with bombs.
>
> But with precision."

Chapter 21 – Shadows Within

January 24, 04:40 hrs IST
Multiple Locations, Suryadesh

The war on the border made the news.
The war inside the country did not.

And that's exactly how **Aarav Sen** wanted it.

Surya Nagar – SIA Black Site Echo-6

A man screamed.

Not for the first time. Not for the last.

His voice was muffled by reinforced walls and drowned beneath the low hum of fluorescent lights.

He was a logistics clerk from the Ministry of Culture.

On paper, he was a mid-level nobody.

But his encrypted calls had pinged three numbers in Turan.
He'd rented an apartment under a false name.
And he had a piece of paper in his wallet that read:

"Leena is real."

05:20 hrs – SIA Counterintelligence Briefing

Aarav stood before a wall of photos.

Some marked. Some burned.
Some still circled in red. **Leena** among them.

"She's still here," he said quietly. "And she's not done."

Mumbai, Sector 12 – 06:11 hrs

A woman stepped off the train.

Blue dupatta. No makeup. Broken sandal.

To anyone watching, she was a tired commuter.
But her hair was a little too neat. Her eyes a little too alert. Her gait too clean for exhaustion.

She passed two posters one calling for blood donations, the other showing a memorial for the Akshepgarh massacre.

Her lips didn't move. But her eyes flicked to both.

Then she turned down a narrow alley.

And vanished.

Leena had escaped the first sweep.

She changed names again. Burned her old ID. Discarded the new one.
She didn't use phones.
She memorised everything.
And she had one instruction left from Zameer:

> "If they find the others, run. If they find you… burn everything behind you."

Across Suryadesh – 09:00 hrs IST

The sweep had begun.

Inland cities. Coastal districts. High-density apartment blocks.

SIA operatives moved with precision some in uniform, some in street clothes.
They cracked caches hidden in government offices.
They pulled flash drives from the walls of prayer halls.
They found encrypted data stored in USBs **taped beneath public benches**.

In Sudhpur, they arrested a radio technician who'd been transmitting phrases in coded Hindi couplets every night.

In Indrapur, they caught a courier disguised as a student handing off what appeared to be poetry notebooks.

Inside were strike coordinates.
Written in verse.

But not all wins felt like victory.

In a sweep near Nalgad, three agents cornered a suspected handler in an abandoned farmhouse.

The man **detonated a pulse bomb**, killing himself and two operatives instantly.

No survivors. No files.
Just silence.

Meanwhile – Bashirat, Al-Bashir

Zameer was briefed.

> "Twelve cells compromised. Fourteen handlers down.
> But Leena escaped."

He smiled.

> "She always does."

He circled one date on his calendar.

Then underlined it.

"And she will be needed very, very soon."

Surya Nagar – 21:50 hrs

Aarav stared at the single photo they had left of her.

It wasn't even real anymore.
Just a ghost of a face.
Of a woman who'd almost stolen a nation's secrets.

"We'll find her," one agent said.

Aarav didn't answer.

He already knew she would **find them first**.

Chapter 22 – Below the Threshold

January 26, 01:10 hrs IST

SIA Black Grid – Undisclosed Location, Suryadesh

Aarav Sen stood before a multi-layered digital projection: a 3D cross-section of Al-Bashir's terrain, glowing like the anatomy of a dying beast.

"These are not guesses," he said.

The room was full of high-clearance operatives from three allied nations. MI6, Mossad, RAW.

He zoomed in.

"We have located seven nuclear bunkers. Three active. Two camouflaged under religious sanctuaries. One in a dried-out oil refinery. And the crown jewel Compound Zero beneath the old Al-Tayir canyon. Forty feet underground. Reinforced by Soviet steel and Al-Bashir's last delusion of glory."

An Israeli agent whispered, "And you want to strike all seven?"

Aarav didn't blink.

"We want to erase the concept of a second option."

Meanwhile – Bashirat State Newsroom

Al-Bashir's national broadcast streamed a holographic general
with perfect teeth and perfectly staged patriotism.

> "We have pushed the Suryadeshis back.
> Their cowardice exposed.
> Their own people rioting.
> Victory is ours blessed by faith and bullet!"

Clips played of old strikes looped and rebranded.

Children waved flags beside rubble. Crowds cheered in front of
paid cameras.
The world outside saw shadows.

Inside?
They only saw **the script**.

Leena – Southern Border, Al-Bashir – 03:35 hrs Local Time

She crossed the desert on foot.

Six men followed. Two women. Silent. Armed. Invisible.

She knew the path. She knew the name to whisper at the checkpoint. She knew which tooth to remove if captured it had a chip inside.

She arrived in Bashirat with blood on her boots and **a hard drive strapped to her thigh.**

By 04:10 hrs, she was seated across from Zameer.

He poured her tea.

She handed him the drive.

> "Tara Mehta," she said. "Real name. Fake names. Account trails.
> Hotel logs. Meeting records.
> And… this."

She placed a smaller chip on the table.

> "Sex footage.

> Timestamps match the Geneva summit."

Zameer didn't smile.

He pressed play.

Then leaned back slowly.

"We'll let them strike.

And then we divide them."

SIA HQ – 06:00 hrs IST

Engineers reviewed radiation dispersal models.

Maps were drawn for underground airflow, water table impact,
and bunker debris analysis.
Every strike had to be surgical.
Every gram of uranium accounted for.

Aarav signed off on **Operation Echo Silence.**

> "Strike ready in 72 hours.
> Unless we're forced to go sooner."

10:00 hrs – Geneva

A high-level official from an "unofficial ally" whispered:

> "You're about to cross a threshold.
> If you do this, the world won't stop you.

> But they'll **never admit** they let you do it."

Aditya responded:

> "Let them blink.
> We'll act."

SIA – Contingency Hall – 23:59 hrs

As the timer ticked toward the strike window, an alert blinked.

RED TRANSMISSION – INTERNAL SECURITY LEAK
LEVEL 5 CLEARANCE BREACH – NAME: Tara Mehta

Aditya and Aarav read the same feed.

Aarav closed his eyes.

Aditya swore under his breath.

And the timer kept ticking.

Chapter 23 – The Trigger

January 28, 03:15 hrs IST

Vajra Command Bunker – Suryadesh

The strike authorisation came with no speech. No anthem. No applause.

Just two signatures.
And one key turned.

"Execute Operation Echo Silence," Aarav said.

A cluster of **hypersonic deep-penetration missiles** launched into black sky.
No one clapped.
No one blinked.

Somewhere underground, a countdown reached zero.

Al-Tayir Canyon, Al-Bashir – 02:10 hrs Local Time

The first warhead drilled through the earth like a spear made of thunder.

Bunker 1 was obliterated.

Bunker 2, destabilised.
Bunker 3, still unknown **its heat signature gone cold two minutes before impact.**

A thermal shockwave rippled through the aquifer system near Compound Zero. The vault cracked emitting a gas plume rich with isotopes.

But the payload stayed sealed.
Just barely.

Minimal radiation. Maximum message.

Bashirat, Al-Bashir – Zameer's Private Chamber

The room shook. Again.

He dropped the glass. It shattered.
Sirens howled across Bashirat.

A colonel burst in, blood trailing from his forehead.

> "All targets hit. Our western silo's ventilation shaft has collapsed. Radiation detected."

Zameer's hands shook.

> "How… how did they know all of them?"

The colonel said nothing.

Because he **didn't** know.

Neither did the rest of the world.

Only one man had the full map.
And he'd just pulled the trigger.

Surya Nagar, Suryadesh – 06:00 hrs IST

Tara Mehta sat at her desk, the leak report in front of her.

> **A sex video.**
> Her bank records.
> Her Geneva hotel logs.

Everything.

She stared at the screen, calm outside, breaking inside.

Aarav entered.

> "We're containing the press fallout."

She didn't look at him.

> "They wanted to shame me before they burned.

Let them try.”

Her hands were steady.

But her career wouldn’t be.

Global Headlines – 07:00 GMT

“Suryadesh Strikes Al-Bashir’s Nuclear Vaults”
“Precision Without Precedent”
“Zameer Calls for Mediation”
**“SIA Chief Unmoved: ‘We only disabled what they
denied existed.’”**

Geneva, Berlin, Washington, even Beijing remained silent.

No condemnation.
No applause.

Only… **quiet calculation.**

The world was watching.
Waiting to see if Zameer would escalate.
Or collapse.

Bashirat – Zameer’s Office – 11:22 hrs Local Time

He stared at the floor.

Three aides were dead.
His missiles were dust.
His last usable base, vaporised.

He looked up at Leena.

> "We need mediation.
> Tell the world we'll talk."

She tilted her head.

> "The world's not answering your calls."

He looked back at the window.

The sky was very blue.

Too blue for anyone to believe he was still in control.

Chapter 24 – Fracture-lines

January 30, 18:10 hrs Local Time
Bashirat, Al-Bashir

The prayer call echoed over a city that didn't answer anymore.

Roads that once buzzed with fanatics now sat thick with silence.
Markets opened late, closed early.
Oil lines ran, but cargo convoys were getting hijacked not by
enemies, but by starving men in Al-Bashir's own provinces.

The war wasn't being lost at the front.
It was bleeding out from the spine.

Zameer's Military Command Chamber – 18:12 hrs

The room was full. But colder than usual.

Twelve of his most senior officers sat before him. Generals, air
chiefs, field operatives.

None smiled.
None saluted.

He walked in, slow and straight-backed, but he felt it.

That stench in the air.

Not betrayal.
Something worse: **disinterest**.

He spoke.

"The next phase is simple. We regroup the northern corridor, evacuate Base Nine, and prepare the blast radius protocols if they strike again."

No one objected.
No one responded.

Until one general raised a hand not like a soldier, but a man in a boardroom.

"With respect, sir… we have no second-phase weapons.

Half the northern corridor has declared martial independence.

The only base left operational… is in Kalat. And it hasn't responded in 48 hours."

Zameer stared at him.

"Then reconfirm the chain of command."

Another general spoke.

"They're not responding because they've stopped
listening."

Elsewhere – Bashirat, Religious Council Chambers

Imam Sharif, once a fierce voice for war, now read from a
different sermon:

"A man who leads must not do so from fire and fear,

but from truth.

And when the truth burns in silence,

the people must speak louder."

It was aired live. Uncut.
The feed wasn't interrupted.

Because no one in the state censorship office **showed up for
work.**

Al-Bashir State Media HQ – 21:30 hrs

An anchor went off-script.

Midway through a standard morale segment, he folded his hands
and said:

"My name is Omar Farouk.
I was told to say our enemies have lost.

But I cannot lie anymore.

It is we… who are burning."

The camera cut. But it was too late.
The clip spread across the dark web in **seven minutes**.

Zameer's Palace – 23:00 hrs

He stood alone.

Windows open.
Whiskey untouched.

The lights in Bashirat twinkled below but fewer than last week.
The air smelled like winter smoke and rust.

He heard it again:

"They've stopped listening."

The words rang like prophecy.

He didn't turn when the aide entered.

"Sir. Five generals missed the emergency council tonight.

And the Foreign Minister… is in Dubai. Asylum request confirmed."

Zameer still didn't move.

"Let them run."

A beat passed.

The aide spoke quietly.

"Some of us aren't running, sir.

Some of us… are waiting."

Chapter 25 – The Knife Inside

January 31, 23:40 hrs IST

Surya Nagar – Old Botanical Sector

A drizzle fell on the cracked pavement as "Suhana Malik" walked past the crumbling iron gates of the decommissioned Ministry of Culture building. A construction board half-hung across the entryway, untouched in years.

She didn't look up at the surveillance cameras.

She had disabled them four minutes ago.

Leena wore plain salwar-kameez. Her hair, black with auburn ends. Her stride casual, but calculated.
She walked with the ease of someone returning home, not infiltrating it.

Inside, she climbed the stairwell in silence.

On the fifth floor, a man was already waiting.

Not an aide.
Not a mid-level mole.

Aarav Sen's former security audit chief.
Dismissed quietly two years ago for "philosophical divergence."

Still on the access list.

Still dangerous.

He handed her a black capsule drive.
No words. Just one breathless sentence:

> "Tara Mehta's sex tape was leaked…
> not from Bashirat.
>
> It was captured by **our own diplomatic surveillance op.**
> Geneva. Room 214A."

Leena blinked once.

> "Who authorised it?"

The man shook his head.

> "No one who left a signature.
> But the uplink… was routed through the PMO."

Karunapur – 22:50 hrs IST

Dusty Café near Sector 8 Rail Station

Karan Pratap stirred his fourth cup of tea.

His press pass lay turned over on the table. No one had asked for it in weeks.

The war had moved beyond journalists.

He watched a muted news channel flicker above the counter: A panel of talking heads, maps of Al-Bashir, glowing threat levels.

It didn't matter anymore. Nothing they said mattered.

Not until a hand dropped an envelope on his table and disappeared before he could look up.

Inside:

- Surveillance photos from Tara Mehta's Geneva hotel.
- A still frame of a ceiling lens—focused, clinical, hidden.
- And a single typed line:

"She's not the only one they watched."

On the back of one photo:

"Room 12. Hotel Prakash. Midnight. Come alone."

Karan looked around the café. No one stared back.
He refolded the envelope, slow.

For the first time in days, he felt like a journalist again.

And for the first time in years, he wasn't sure he wanted to know.

Tara Mehta's Office – SIA Internal Vault

She sat alone, her face bathed in the flicker of the monitor.

She had seen the eight leaked clips. Humiliation wrapped in politics.

But now… this.

Clip Nine.

Grainy. High-angle. Fixed.
The entire scene, captured from above not a camera in the room.

A ceiling lens. Hidden behind a thermal vent.

She checked the timestamp.

Geneva Summit.
The exact night. The exact minute.

Then she saw the file tag:
"Orchid-214A. DPG Internal Archive."

DPG. Diplomatic Protocol Group. Suryadesh's own global surveillance wing.

Tara stood up so fast her chair fell.

"It wasn't Zameer," she whispered. "It was… us."

She staggered backward, her face white.

She had spent the last three weeks trying to manage her shame. Now she knew it was **engineered**.

Someone inside wanted her **broken**.
To destabilise the PM. To distract Aarav.
To put her in the crosshairs **not by accident** but by design.

SIA Command Chamber – 00:05 hrs

Aarav Sen sat in silence.

The wall screen glowed with four rotating satellite feeds.

One of them tracked a convoy **crossing the Western Badlands**, just inside Al-Bashir.

The heat signature was unusual. Shielded.
A custom containment layer.

Unmarked.

Military-grade, but unregistered.

He zoomed in.

A tactical AI flagged it:

> "**Nuclear mass anomaly** – Type C. Origin: Unknown."

Aarav frowned.

> "That's not from their remaining stockpile.
> We destroyed every known vault."

His aide stammered.

> "Then this is… something new?"

Aarav nodded.

> "Or something borrowed."

Bashirat – Subterranean Strategic Shelter, 00:40 hrs

Zameer stared at the holo-feed of military defections.

Three provincial bases had declared "operational neutrality."

His empire was **cracking beneath him**.

Behind him, a door hissed open.

His daughter, **Asiya**, entered silently.
In her hands: a sleek, black carbon case.

She placed it on the war table.

"What is that?" he asked.

She opened it.

Inside: a **fission core. Cold. New. Untraced**.

Zameer stepped back.

"Where did this come from?"

She didn't blink.

"Not you.

Someone else. Someone who thinks you're too soft. Too
slow."

"Who?"

She smiled faintly.

"The people who want this war finished, not managed."

"This isn't yours to control," he growled.

She leaned in.

"Neither was the sex tape.
Neither was Geneva.

You were just the opening act."

SIA Comms – 01:00 hrs IST

A transmission came through on a secure line.

But it didn't match any internal call pattern.

It was routed through a dead protocol: **Black Daffodil**.

Only one agent had ever used that.

Leena's original handler.

The message?

"Phase Two is green. The knife is already inside."

Final Lines – Tara Mehta's Quarters

Tara stared at the screen.

The last leaked image showed not her.
But the man walking away from the diplomatic suite in Geneva.

He had clearance.
He had the PM's trust.
And she recognised him.

Her voice shook as she whispered the name.

"No… not him."

Undisclosed – The Journalist's Field Notebook

Entry marked: Feb 1, 02:12 hrs

They told us this war would be fought with fire.
But it's being fought with silence.
With edits. With clipped soundbites. With footage that can't be
verified until the next body is found.

I saw the blast craters. I smelled the ash.

But the things I'm seeing now—
The ones whispered in parking lots, tucked in sealed folders,
handed over in exchange for nothing but eye contact—

They're louder than the bombs.

If I vanish, tell them I was right.

And tell them: the truth died last.

— Karan Pratap

AUTHOR BIO

Dr. Subin Mathews is a storyteller, strategist, and observer of power, both visible and hidden. With a background in engineering and science, and a passion for realism and global affairs, he brings his characters to life with moral tension, precision, and a cinematic eye.

War Without Orders is his debut political thriller and the first entry in The Order Protocols series. He lives in India, surrounded by books, ideas, and the quiet hum of unfinished stories.

COMING SOON – Ashes of Order

The war isn't over.
The world just stopped looking.

In the sequel to War Without Orders, new enemies emerge—not from across the border, but from inside the corridors of power. As a rogue nuclear device inches toward deployment, alliances fracture, spy networks collapse, and Suryadesh must decide whether it can still trust itself.

Book Two: Ashes of Order – Coming Late 2025